SNOW DAY

Based on the episode "Henry and the Sno-Grrr," written by Colm Tyrrell
Adapted by Bill Scollon
Illustrated by Premise Entertainment

ABDOBOOKS.COM

Reinforced library bound edition published in 2019 by Spotlight, a division of ABDO, PO Box 398166, Minneapolis, Minnesota 55439. Spotlight produces high-quality reinforced library bound editions for schools and libraries. Published by agreement with Disney Press, an imprint of Disney Book Group.

Printed in the United States of America, North Mankato, Minnesota.
092018   012019

DⁱꜱɴᴇY PRESS
New York • Los Angeles

THIS BOOK CONTAINS
RECYCLED MATERIALS

Library of Congress Control Number: 2017961155

Publisher's Cataloging-in-Publication Data

Names: Scollon, Bill, author. | Tyrrell, Colm, author. | Premise Entertainment, illustrator.
Title: Henry Hugglemonster: Snow day / by Bill Scollon and Colm Tyrrell; illustrated by Premise Entertainment.
Description: Minneapolis, MN : Spotlight, 2019 | Series: World of reading level pre-1
Summary: Henry and Beckett want to go sledding on Mount Roarsmore, but Henry's friends are scared of the legendary Snow-Grr that lives on top of the mountain.
Identifiers: ISBN 9781532141805 (lib. bdg.)
Subjects: LCSH: Henry Hugglemonster (Television program)--Juvenile fiction. | Winter--Juvenile fiction. | Sledding--Juvenile fiction. | Abominable snowman--Juvenile fiction. | Readers (Primary)--Juvenile fiction.
Classification: DDC [E]--dc23

Spotlight
A Division of ABDO
abdobooks.com

Henry loves the snow!
He wants to go sledding.
Beckett loves the snow.
He will go, too.

Mount Roarsmore is huge.
Henry's sled will go fast!

Summer wants to go sledding, too.

But their friends are afraid.
What are they afraid of?
Estelle throws up her arms.
"A big, scary Snow-Grrr!"

"Don't worry," says Henry.
"Snow-Grrrs are not real."

Summer sees a big footprint!

Estelle screams!
"It's from the Snow-Grrr!"

But Henry is not scared.
"Snow-Grrrs are not real."

11

The ground begins to shake!
Stomp, stomp, stomp.

"The Snow-Grrr!" shouts Denzel.

Henry does not think so.
"It must be something else."

A booming voice laughs.
"Ha, ha, ha!"

Henry's friends want to go home!
Henry does not.

The snow is perfect.
Henry wants to go sledding.

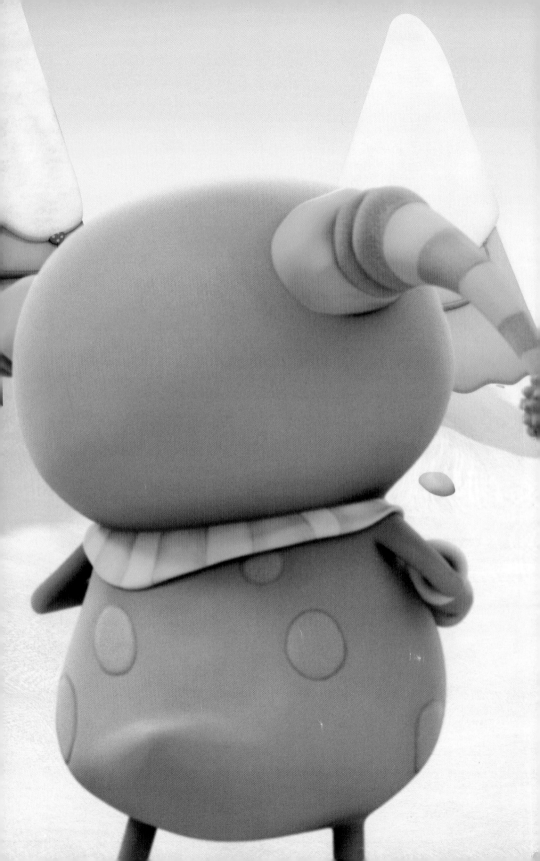

The friends climb Mount Roarsmore.
They see a big shadow!
Is it the Snow-Grrr?

Henry goes to find out.
Beckett goes with him.

A giant hand grabs Henry and
Beckett!

It is not a Snow-Grrr.
It is Estelle's dad,
Mr. Enormomonster!

Henry was right.

There is no Snow-Grrr!

Henry can't wait to tell his friends.

Mr. and Mrs. Enormomonster have
been busy.
They have a surprise.

Estelle's parents made snow monsters!
Gertie smiles.
"They look just like us!"

Summer loves her snow monster.
"She is fabulous!"

It is time to go sledding!
Mr. Enormomonster gives Henry
a push.

"ROARSOME!"